An Interview With Failure

AN INTERVIEW WITH FAILURE

SAM YANKELEVITCH

Having done our best to tell a truthful story, this is nonetheless a work of fiction. Unless otherwise indicated, all the names, characters, avatars, memes, businesses, places, events and incidents in this book are either the product of the author's misguided imagination and/or used in a fictitious manner. Any resemblance to actual persons, demons, witches, ogres, living or dead, or actual events is purely coincidental.

The content of this book is for entertainment and informational purposes only and is not intended to diagnose, aggravate, transmit, treat, cure, or prevent any condition or disease. You understand that this book is not intended as a substitute for consultation with a therapist or other licensed practitioner. Please consult with your own physician or healthcare specialist regarding the suggestions and recommendations made in this book. The use of this book implies your acceptance of this disclaimer.

Although the author and publisher have made every effort to ensure that the information in this book was correct at press time, the book is about Failure, thus imperfection should be expected and accepted.

The publisher and the author are providing this book and its contents on an "as is" basis with the probability of imperfections, errors, inaccuracies, omissions, weird s . . . t, and other potential inconsistencies.

Grateful appreciation:

A very special THANKS to friends and family who took the time to read early manuscripts and who provided invaluable corrections, feedback and ideas for improvement: Sherri Junkins, Nancy Gooch, Liz Guthridge, Jim Thompson, Marcel Sanchez, Daniela Mathews, Myriam Cohen, Schelly Levy (Mom).

Feedback, Friendship and Family: some good F words.

"There are more things . . . likely to frighten us than there are to crush us; we suffer more in imagination than in reality."

Seneca

In the spring of 2018, Robin Finch, a young influencer, set up an interview with Failure on the "Wake Up and Leap Forward" podcast.

By the end of the podcast, the listeners were suddenly ready to take the first step.

After pulling back the curtain, absent fear, they quickly stumbled on success.

They had stopped walking in the shadow of other people's words.

Interview:
Part 1

Hello everyone and welcome to the 87th episode of Wake Up and Leap Forward a podcast created to get people like yourself to realize there are many perspectives out there you can learn from and that you are not just one story.

In the past weeks, I've been reviewing the feedback and questions I get from you, my listeners, and one of the themes that seems to repeat quite a bit is the feeling of fear people have about failing.

As I looked deeper into your feedback, the fear is biggest when thinking about taking action, and that first step.

So, for today's episode, I've invited a very special guest, the ultimate source of knowledge on this subject.

I've invited Failure to today's conversation.

Plenty has been written, there are books and seminars out there, TED talks and advice everywhere, and yet fear of Failure is still very present for many. So, I thought that perhaps having Failure, on my show, we could get to a more fundamental understanding, pull back the curtain and see what this is really all about?

I'm thinking that if we can provide our listeners with information directly from the source, they can see things from a different perspective that can help them move forward.

So, let's get started.

Hello Failure, thank you for coming on my show to talk to me and my listeners.

—No problem, Robin.

To be honest, I was not really sure you'd make it. I suppose you're always so busy ha ha , so I really did not know what to expect.

—On my own I'm not really that busy. But I get it. For you humans, the busy chatter, doubting, worrying and forming expectations, I mean, that's kind of normal.

I guess so. I make a lot of assumptions. Like all the time. But I really appreciate you taking the time. I'm trying to reflect a bit on my own projects and the types of questions I'm getting from the listeners to my show. And I suppose life in general too.

I prepared a few questions to bounce off you. Can we start?

—Sure. Jump right in. Let's have fun.

Cool. So. I'm thinking about the problem first. When thinking about doing something, making a decision, for many people, for whatever reason, your name pops up. It's as if your name is always hovering around and putting pressure on me. Like I'm being watched or something. I was wondering how you do that? How do you manage to float around like that? You seem to be an expert at it.

—An expert? Hah hah. Thank you for the compliment. Floating and hovering is actually quite easy for ideas and thoughts. They are weightless in the physical world. So I guess the expertise is innate. It's inherent to what I am and what I do. And the hovering you describe, well, therein lies the answer to your question.

I'm not at fault.

Not sure I understand it all. Your name is not weightless. In my case, and what my friends say about you does weigh. And quite heavily, any time we need to choose, make a decision to do something we have not done before.

Just the thought of your name carries a load. Fear, shame, humiliation. Sometimes it just mortifies and bears tremendous guilt.

Surely you can take some responsibility for the heavy load? How could you not?

—Well since you ask, I'll make it easy for you Robin. I can't take responsibility at all. I'm just a word. That's all I am.

—S I L E N C E—

—Hello? Robin, are you on mute?

Oh . . . no no. I'm here. It's just. Well. I guess I'll have to get clear on what you mean. Just a word? I feel that there is more to that. I've never really considered failure just a word.

Maybe we can start again?

—Robin, when you invited me to the interview, we did no clarify up front what I am. It's never too late though.

Like I said, I am a word. A tool. A device. A component of what you call language.

What I know is that for you and your buddies to do things together, you need devices like me to understand each other. There are thousands of tools like me out there, and each tool is supposed to be useful for a specific purpose.

Guess what, you've pretty much invented my kind, words, to coordinate and inter-act with others.

Yes, but I think you've taken advantage of your status.

There is a power about you.

I can tell you that the feelings you evoke are not pleasant. I told you, you can mortify me, sometimes you make me afraid to do things, or make choices.

—I'll stick to my story Robin. I'm just a word. And by the way, on another call, someone mentioned the "sticks and stones" rhyme, I think it helped make the conversation move forward a bit — do you know it?

Do you mean, "sticks and stones can break my bones, but words will never hurt me"? I see. This is something that my teachers in school taught us to deflect when other kids called us names. But to tell you the truth, that didn't work very well. I remember feeling humiliated and angry either way with the name calling. But since then, I haven't given it much thought.

Let me think though. Nothing's changed. Words can in fact hurt. It's still true. Sticks and stones can break my bones, and words can also hurt me. Shouldn't it change?

—Oh. Yes, change for sure, but the change should happen elsewhere. Let me try something different. Ok?

OK.

—Remember I compared what I am "a word" with a tool. Tools like hammers or knives might have been first made by humans to accomplish a special task. To hammer in other stones to build a home, or knives for cutting up plants or animals. Let's say that was many years ago.

Then circumstances changed, societies and communities grew, and today knives and hammers are being used in so many different ways. Doctor's use hammers and knives in surgery. Oh, and they also use small rubber hammers on knees to check for reflexes, ha ha.

Or take the wheel for example. As a tool. Maybe with

the original purpose to help carry objects or people from point A to point B. And wheels have so many other purposes today: they can be small gears to make other gears move, steering wheels on cars and ships.

Tools might have had an original purpose, a specific need at the time they were conceived, but as the world constantly evolves and circumstances change, the purpose of a tool can also change.

That's an interesting idea. What you're saying is that based on the need, one can change the purpose of a knife or a wheel. In your case though, as a word, your purpose is already pre-defined. You just used the example of the wheel to "carry" objects and in you case, you carry a meaning. That is the way you serve a common purpose where I and my buddies can communicate. By agreeing on the meaning you carry as a word.

So, the tool explanations kind of make sense for tools. But for words I think it's different, it's not making sense?

—As I said before, I'm just a word Robin. I don't carry anything and if you're talking about meanings, meanings are carried by humans, not by words.

"When *I* use a word," Humpty Dumpty said, in rather a scornful tone, "it means just what I choose it to mean — neither more nor less."

"The question is," said Alice, "whether you *can* make words mean so many different things."

"The question is," said Humpty Dumpty, "which is to be master — that's all."

Lewis Carroll,
Through the Looking Glass

Interview:
Part 2

Can you explain a bit?

—Look, if you ask your child to clean their room and then check their room, after they said they're done, what might you find? Maybe they picked up their clothes from the floor and put their toys in a box. But if they left pizza crumbs on the floor, and a sticky leftover stain from their soda on their nightstand, did they really clean the room?

To them, they carried their own meaning of *clean*, and you carried your own meaning, even though the word *clean* is a simple word we use every day. Does this help?

Wait wait. The meanings I'm talking about are written in the dictionary. Or I can look up words on Google and the meanings will pop up. When I look you up, the meanings are spelled out and explained. And based on what the dictionary says, my buddies and I can agree on the meaning and have a conversation.

Otherwise, if as you say we each carry a meaning, then how do we agree what a word means. Would be tough to talk with others and be on the same page? I kind of get what you're trying to explain about me carrying the meaning, not a word.

But then how should we relate to the meanings in a dictionary?

—That's a good question. If you don't mind, I'll share a brief history about myself. I think it will help illustrate what I'm about and clarify my role as a word.

Since you mentioned a dictionary, I'll talk about that, but you have to keep in mind that long before dictionaries there were other ways by which people and other natural beings communicated. At a certain point in history humans developed symbols to use as ways to share information. They agreed on what specific symbols and sounds meant. Eventually symbols evolved into words, and dictionaries were devised with the intent to capture the meanings of words, so they could be used for people to inter-act.

Specifically, my name was given to me in English sometime around the 1600 or 1700 as far as I can recall. Which is not too long ago, considering humans have used language way before then.

My name was originally French, set as *faillir* in one of the first dictionaries ever published. I'm not sure how the people in charge of collecting words into a volume came up with the actual sound and spelling, but I suspect they were all very educated and knowledgeable

I also suspect that they were grumpy old men.

I mean really, think of the tasks and the work and the times. How many women were well educated then? Most were assigned to taking care of the home. Knowledge of linguistics was often limited to few experts that could spend the time to study words, their origins and their meanings.

Remember also that at the time my name was set in the dictionary, Latin was thought of as a common language and so, many word names in English somehow have a Latin source. And also, Greek or German sometimes. So many words in the English dictionary were derived from other languages.

Hold on. Sorry. I intended to be brief, but I want my explanation to be as useful as possible. OK?

Yes, please go on.

—When these guys decided to add my name to their list of words, they selected only a few meanings. But the original French word had so many more descriptions for my name. So many ways to interpret. However, they narrowed down the definitions and limited the choices.

Maybe you can later share a more complete list of meanings with your listeners Robin.

I still believe that what they discussed about *faillir*, was meant to have a positive connotation, as an opportunity, a gap to be filled. Perhaps for people to look at my name and think how something could be improved. That a task committed to could be finished, completed. Or, perhaps for someone to not have to pay compensation for a task not done according to an expectation, whether incomplete or wrong. It alluded to an opportunity for asking for a corrective, a reparation. Something not finished or not done.

By the way, it could be that some of the same grumpy old men defining the meanings of words were influenced by their religious beliefs. Think how in those days there a lot of discussion was about what was sinful, what was right or wrong, good or bad.

Words, and their meanings, were probably influenced by the prevailing mindset of the times, so, perhaps part of *faillir* could be associated with right and wrong. Or even what is sinful, or not. The important part is that based on their own preference, they ignored other possible meanings.

Do you follow Robin? Is this too much information?

No, yes. It's quite interesting.

Many of my listeners focus on one single definition because most of our English dictionaries limited the meanings to just a few. Might not be the best influence.

But I think what you're alluding to is that the meanings in the dictionary were set by certain folks, in certain circumstances. And it's interesting that you mention the original French version, with particular intended meanings.

I think the meanings of your name today are even more different.

—Well, that is a key point that I'd like to bring across.

When circumstances change, the meaning of a word can also change. Remember I'm just a tool. Meanings are very relevant to the conditions around the time they were agreed to. To be useful and serve a group of people based on their needs then.

So, if the need changes, one can adapt and use the tool in a different way.

Yes. That makes sense. I'm not sure how your name evolved from French to English, I guess I can look it up later.

But what I think is that the English version does not always come off as a positive. It's associated with the idea of being incompetent, a loser, or defeated. And it's like an absolute idea, an either or. Either fail or succeed. There's no in-between. No opening to as you said, to correct something or offer compensation.

Maybe my thinking is also based on the circumstances of when I first heard the word. And I re-call it was not a very positive situation. For example, I heard an aunt tell my dad how he was a failure. Maybe she even said, total failure. Some of my teachers in school also told kids that they were failures, when they did not give a correct answer to a question.

Thinking back these were vey judgmental people, but nonetheless the word stuck with me in a negative sense, an either or, black and white, the opposite of success.

I guess this is also why I wanted to talk to you. Many of my listeners have asked questions about ways to improve and be successful, and your name always comes up as an obstacle.

Do you have any suggestions?

—I think I do. I would start with the last thing you mentioned about success and my name. It's like saying that black and white are opposites when in fact each color has its own properties.

White is a name given to a particular color with a hue that reflects light completely and disperses it all. Black is a name given to a color that lacks hue and absorbs all light without reflecting any light rays.

Even though they're two distinct shades of color, each with their own characteristics, often they are thought of as opposites to one another. But the written descriptions relate to extremes, where either all light gets reflected or zero light gets reflected.

Have you seen snow? You say it's *white*, but it reflects only 70–80% of light, not all. And most surfaces you call *black*, also reflect some light depending on the type and finish of the surface.

The point is to not confuse the proposed written meanings with absolute ideas.

The way these colors are used in language to compare with a situation has created the false impression that they are actual opposites. Might be useful in some situations, but not useful in all.

Just because it's written in a book doesn't mean it's true.

Which relates to your question Robin:

People think that success and my name are opposites, but this is really not so. The two words can be related; however they do not necessarily represent the flip side of the other.

Success can mean different things to different people. To some it can be money. To others it's health, family or good friends.

Does this help?

Sure, it's an interesting point of view. I personally think that "having spare time" is a great measure of success, especially if it's used to learn and help others. Yet my typical listener is more interested in money as a measure of success, although a few do talk about family.

It's like the saying that the grass is always greener on the other side, is an incorrect comparison. Perhaps the grass is different on the other side, but not necessarily better or worse.

Besides, it's tough to know what is really beneath the face of the success we perceive in others. When we are highlighting only the good, at the same time we're ignoring the mistakes they may have made along the way. Or the internal struggles they still carry.

I guess you're suggesting pondering a bit more on how we define success as well as keeping that definition independent of your name?

—That could be one way. There may be other ways too. But the principle behind this is about what you stated just now about different preferences and points of view.

It's a matter of individual perspective.

You can choose to view things your own unique way, and based on your particular attitude and intent you will get different responses.

So, if you really inspect a word more closely, you might find a way for it to be useful to you, and helpful in your quest toward success.

Whatever you define success to mean for you.

It is your choice, if you want to stop walking in the shadow of other people's words.

Walking in the shadow of other people's words? interesting, I had never heard that before. Thank you. I'll write that one down.

"Be yourself, everyone else is already taken."

Oscar Wilde

Interview:
Part 3

Thanks again for those great thoughts.

Let's talk more about words. I think you said that when circumstances change, and needs change, the meanings of words can also change?

—Yes. and let me also add that new words are also constantly being created by people. Some end up in dictionaries and some don't.

Let me give you some examples. Recently I was on another interview, and I heard people say *yolo* and things being *ratched*. These words were being used by many younger folks and when I asked, they said *yolo* meant "you only live once" and ratched, "something or someone vile or nasty".

But back when I was named, and put in a dictionary, these words did not exist. Google did not exist either, and now google is a common word that can be a noun or a verb, like *googling* something or someone.

I'll bet you anything that the people listening to this interview know a bunch of words that started to be used a short time ago. How these get invented or named can be a matter of a popular song or movie where the word is mentioned and then all it takes is for people to share it and start using it.

As you can see there can be an endless stream of words that enter the vocabulary.

I really had not given that too much thought. I guess I'm distanced from some generations and too much in my own little world. But I can see also how many new words can enter our vocabulary with globalization which is accelerating. Just with foods for example, I remember growing up we would scoff at the idea of eating raw fish. To use your word, that would have been *ratched*, ha ha. But today we eat sushi and even in supermarkets there is sushi everywhere.

Same raw fish, new name, new perspective.

Come to think of it, pop culture might be a good source of words. Rappers can be quite influential in promoting words that were never used before, or did not exist before. And then their fans acquire those words and start using them in their daily interactions with others.

The other day someone I was talking with responded to me and said *cap*. I was kind of startled and had to ask what that was.

Turns out people started using *cap* to mean lie or BS. They explained *no cap* means for real. I guess I was being told I'm a *capper,* a liar. I did google the word the other day, and it's a word that is being widely used by new generations.

I'm sure there are hundreds or even thousands of new words being created all the time, as things are changing so fast.

—That's probably true, I've seen some new names pop up.
So, the idea is that we can create new words, acquire

new words from other parts of the world or even invent our own definition of an existing word.

The important thing to keep in mind is that it is up to us to keep the meaning useful, use the word as a tool to take care of a need, to help you do something.

That's when your attitude matters.

Once you realize you can choose the meaning of a word, wouldn't you choose one that is helpful and positive?

Choosing an attitude. That in itself is an activity right? I'd have to define exactly what attitude I should take on, so it can help me invent a meaning that is useful for my needs. Does this sound like a path forward to help solve the fear and negative association with failure? Any tips on doing this?

—Definitely Robin. You're on the right track. I have suggested people could simply change their relationship with words.

Yes, like with other people, pets or valuables, people can have a relationship with a word. Without a relationship the meaning of a word itself is transactional, rigid, like an agreement that cannot be renegotiated. Changing that relationship can be a first step that will help you move forward by establishing a relationship that is more flexible and deliberate.

I like that analogy a lot. The relationship with a word and having a more flexible way of thinking about the meanings, so we can take control, instead of being controlled.

—That can be a good reinforcement of attitude to change the relationship with words which helps with the next step, which is defining your own meaning for a word that is not serving you well.

Make it a tool that works for you, not against you.

Yes, in fact over the years we choose the friends we keep and sometimes let go of those that are judgmental or unreliable. We decide who we spend our time with. Sometimes you have to let go of friends.

I guess it could be the same with our relationship with a word that is not useful any longer.

—Robin, have you heard the story of the two frogs?

I don't think so, what is it?

—Here goes:

A band of frogs was traveling in the dark of night and two of them fell into a deep well.

At dawn, the frogs above the well counseled the two frogs, yelling that there was no hope, the well was too deep.

They loudly recommended they should give it up and not waste their energy trying to escape.

However, deep in the well, the two frogs proceeded with more than a few attempts to leap out.

One of two frogs got tired and gave up.

The other frog kept trying: leaping and learning.

The frogs atop wondered why this frog was still leaping, and continued to shout their advice, to just give up.

Finally, one of the experiments worked for the trapped frog, and leaping higher, it finally made it out.

When the rest of the band asked: "Did you not hear us?", the frog replied:

"Not really, I could not hear what you were yelling, I have a hearing problem. Actually, I thought you were encouraging me and cheering me on."

What is the moral of this story? you can always turn a deaf ear to the inner critic.

Other people's words can prevent you from leaping out, if you let them seep into your mind.

I love it, I'm pretty sure our listeners will remember this story, it's great.

Going back to the knife analogy, it could be like choosing to make it the surgeon's knife that saves lives instead of a dagger that can stab you in the back? I'm thinking that the sharp edge will be similar in each case, but we could take responsibility and choose the shape of the blade and the type of handle. Think how a small blade and handle is useful for a surgeon, and a heavy handle and blade for a hunter.

We can each deliberately create a tool that is intended for a specific need and make it useful for that need.

—That's a good one Robin, or you can even make up a completely new word that can help you be more in tune with your own unique idea of what the tool should do for you.

I like it. I think this would be a great challenge for the people listening to this interview. Maybe later we open a contest and hear what words they invent.

If they invent a meaning that is useful to them, then they would deliberately be choosing to not be walking in the shadow of someone else's words.

—Exactly Robin.

By the way, I know you're the one asking the questions, but I just remembered a question that might be helpful to strengthen this idea for your listeners.

It's a story from the Buddha, asking someone "If you Robin, were to buy a gift for someone and that person decides to not receive it, to whom does the gift belong?"

Well, if they choose to not receive it, I guess it would belong to me, Right?

—**Exactly. So, to your sticks and stones rhyme earlier, if one uses a word to judge someone and that someone decides to not receive it because the word is not useful to them, or doesn't match how they define it, then words could not hurt that person.**

If a judgment doesn't stick to a person, then who does the judgement belong to?

"Our view of the world is truly shaped by what we decide to hear."

William James

Interview:
Part 4

Hmm, I think putting that together with what we were discussing earlier about choosing a meaning that is useful for each of us, can be even more effective for anyone trying to get away from the negative associations with your name. Can you share any ideas or maybe other stories that can help guide our listeners on how to choose a more useful meaning?

—Yes, let's talk about stories a bit. If you were to agree that words are made up.

That their meaning are set by others, from their own unique perspective. Perhaps it was helpful for them, in their case, in their conditions, circumstances and context. In their world.

Just because you had been ignoring it was someone else's world does not mean it wasn't active and alive in your head. Their meaning may have slipped into your mind, and hijacked your voice. Then who's voice was behind the self-talk you thought was yours?

Listen, there's no need to blame others. Assume they had positive intent, perhaps to protect you from external influences.

Now, it's time to shift.

Think back, how you yanterpreted my name? What was your context? Under what circumstances did you integrate the meaning into your life?

What were you feeling? Seeing? Hearing?

What story did you tell yourself then? What details did you leave out?

You are not just one story.

It's time to edit, find more choices, different meanings, different worlds, get unstuck and move forward.

Those old stories, with the old meanings may have been useful to you in the past. But what if those old meanings have become obsolete?

Cool, I think I get it. You're suggesting that if someone is not authoring their own story, maybe they are letting someone else author it for them? And, once we grasp this, we can start editing our own story, one that better suits us.

I guess this is where choosing meanings deliberately really counts.

This is what I've learned over the years: as humans, we act based on how we think, and we think based on how we see. But we see based on what we believe to be true.

And primarily we believe, based on what we repeat to ourselves in our heads, over and over.

Communication is such a hot topic, mainly because we are still learning how to communicate with others. And when we need to get things done, we first have to communicate. What has to get done, by who, by when.

In that sense, we can say that communication precedes, or rather pre-seeds action.

In other words, the seed for getting things done lies silently inside communication.

Since we also communicate with ourselves, and words, or rather their meanings, weigh heavily in this process, we can improve how we communicate with ourselves and influence how we take the first step.

The voice in our heads uses words that seed the conditions by which we will act in the physical world. These words tell us what we will do, how will do it, when we will do it.

Maybe we can reflect on the words and meanings we chose when we talk to ourselves, and how they influenced our actions and our progress. When we realize what words created doubt and confusion about the what, the how and the when, we have a choice.

So, we should strive to nurture the seed, that pre-seeds our actions to be useful, and not work against us.

—Nice addition Robin: words pre-seed action. It's like you plant a seed that builds your world with words and then those words shape your world.

The good thing is you don't have to follow conventions, especially if they are no longer helping you.

Like in the story of little David and giant Goliath.

How could David have won the battle?

I suspect David was one of the first language rebels.

He was young and had learned how to win by breaking made-up rules and conventions.

While old Goliath had everyone thinking the only way to fight was with a sword, David chose his own tool, one that was useful to him, a slingshot.

What if you could win by breaking a convention of words? By choosing your own meaning of a word.

Swords or words: why not choose a meaning about my name that will give you an edge?

Wow, that is a cool way of seeing a story from the Bible.

—Yes, I think it might help your listeners.

Now, how about we make it personal to you Robin. Would it be OK to talk a bit about what you do? Together we might come up with other ideas to guide others.

Sure, what do you have in mind?

—Well, when we first spoke about the interview you told me that we would just get on a virtual call, and you would be recording this and then you would edit the recording before making it public. So, I assume sometimes you edit parts of an interview out?

Yes, that is right. I can go into the video and cut parts out or add things to make the video look better. For this interview for example we will just chat and if anything is not needed, or if you want me to edit out something of the interview, I can do that.

Another thing is when I produce an online class. These are filmed and produced as videos. I have to write out a script for each lesson and then I shoot each lesson in front of a camera. After I finish shooting all the lessons then I go in to edit.

—How do you to keep track of each lesson? When you're watching each lesson how do you know where you might have to add, or cut out part of the video?

Good question. Something that helps a lot is what they call a clapper board. That board that we see on TV where someone says: take one, take three, take 10.

On a film set you'll hear: rolling, sound, slate, action. The slate is another way they call the clapper. Each take is numbered on the clapper board and filmed at the beginning of the take, which then helps find the specific location on a video that can be cut out or edited to add titles, sound or other things.

—I have seen those clapper boards. I love it when they say the take number and the sound it makes when they

snap it closed, Scene 4, Take 12 and roll. I'm thinking that each time the clapper claps, is a take that sometimes has to be repeated because something was not 100%? I assume that since humans are involved, there are problems with the lighting, background noise, or when you're reading a script and pronounced a word wrong or missed a word or didn't smile enough.

Think about it, you could refer to any take that is not 100% as a missed-take.

You know that there will always be a chance to make another take until it's right.

Do you see how this can apply to our conversation about my name? Instead of thinking about a big, fatalistic, end of the world idea, it can be a missed-take, or simply a mistake?

Hey, I've been doing this for a very long time, and never associated my clapper board with mistakes.

Thank you for this idea.

Now that you mention it, I guess whoever invented this device had lots of situations with missed-takes and decided to keep track and number them somehow. It makes it easy to refer back to take 1 or take 6 and learn something about the lighting, the sound, how the actor looked or any other detail that seems off.

The loud CLACK! sound can be a good reminder for all of

us that each action, is just a take. That we have the power to pause and a chance to edit and get many do overs before we're happy with the result.

—Sounds like you have lots of fun Robin when shooting your videos. Because you knew that any missed-takes could be fixed, it didn't seem to worry you a lot. Maybe just a small frustration or disappointment that things were going to take a bit more time than planned. That is an attitude.

Don't you think the clapper opened a space? A way to pause and control how you reacted to a mistake?

That is true. And I must say that it's important to consider that when I film there are so many variables: the equipment, the room noise, the natural lights from the sun, people's skills and emotions. And so many more that I cannot control.

By the way, we sometimes use the actual footage of some bad takes to watch and laugh, as we learn. We refer to these as bloopers. Maybe we can use the idea and add a new F word: Floopers?

—That's funny. Maybe it will be added beside my name one day.

I was thinking of another idea about the invention of

the clapper. You could use it to set the idea that perfection does not exist.

One of the issues people have with my name is that they somehow believe perfection exists. That belief then is what they compare their actions with which in turn drives disappointment and fear. Believing in perfection helps create a false expectation that things are linear when in reality life is curvy. Such false beliefs help set you up for disappointment by associating your actions with my name.

By realizing that perfection is an illusion, it can help transform the belief of perfection into a more useful idea that can help people become less afraid.

If as they say, change is a constant, how can perfection survive?

Each loud CLACK of the clapper means you're moving one step in the right direction.

That's very good. We need to keep on moving because even though there is a final cut to produce the show, we always find something we could improve on for the next episode.

"Experience is merely the name
men gave to their mistakes."

Oscar Wilde

Interview:
Part 5

That was very valuable info, thank you for sharing. I'm sure the listeners are getting something good from your responses.

Hey, a while back I was very interested in learning about meditation and one of the teachers told me something that has stuck with me for many years.

It's this simple phrase: "expectation reduces joy."

When I get into disappointing situations, I try to remember this. I guess it's one way to avoid falling into the trap of believing in perfection.

—*Expectation reduces joy.* So now I learned a good one from you Robin.

For sure, perfection is similar to other illusions. It can exist in someone's mind, but think about it, if perfection implies something thoroughly complete, or flawless then how and where would we fit change?

Physically we see change happening all the time, plants growing, people getting old, the ocean never stops changing its form, the earth is alive, and life means change. Maybe it's human thing to cling or attach to something that is not changing, something to help anchor a moment. I understand the need. But the clinging probably leads to more disappointment, frustration.

Change is indeed constant. Can you elaborate a bit more, or maybe give another example that the listeners can use to avoid disappointment?

—Ok. think of something that you plan. You can write the plan down with as many details as you want. But chances are things will not go 100% according to your plan when there are many variables involved, and things you have no control over: the weather, other people, unexpected global pandemics, mother nature.

One way to picture this is by drawing out the plan as a straight line. But when the plan meets the real world, the line gets curvy and curly.

If in your mind you stick with the illusion of a straight line, wouldn't the curvy stuff create disappointment?

Think about this, if you compare a perfectly straight line or flat line to a horizontal line, associated with the horizon, the line where the earth's surface appears to meet the sky, is that not also an illusion?

Next time you look out there, try to find precisely where that horizon line is perfect.

I think it's more the doing of humans trying to make sense of things and labeling them to satisfy a need.

Nonetheless, a label of "straight", "flat" or "perfect" does not make the physical object straight, flat or perfect.

If the horizon is an illusion, does perfect exist?

That is really cool.

It's interesting how we use and believe the term "nobody's perfect" but then don't really apply that to situations or outcomes of our work. With what you're saying, no one is perfect, not because of them, but because perfection does not exist.

Knowing this helps avoid that paralyzing feeling knowing we cannot achieve something. It really clarifies that *perfect* is not the target of what we do. It makes more sense to focus on learning from our progress with each action we take, instead of focusing so much on the end result. If perfection is an illusion, then there really is no point in waiting for the "perfect" condition to get started and taking the first step.

Here's a question:

Since some of our listeners carry the fear of your name when they compare an outcome of their actions when things don't come out perfect and they feel bad. Do you think it would make sense to choose an anchor to remind us of this reality, that *perfect* doesn't exist?

—Depends on what your meaning for anchor is Robin. For example, a ship drops an anchor to keep it in one place. Secure, and safe. If safety is the choice, you'd think the anchor worked. That is the plan at least.

But many things can still fail. Rough seas, and storms can still move the ship around, out of its intended secure

area. And once the anchor is thrown into the water you don't know what it has hit to attach to, if at all.

Below the surface is an unknown.

So perhaps a better idea for using an anchor is to remember as you're throwing it, to not set an expectation that everything will be 100%?

The moment someone is going to take action, they are throwing an anchor below the surface of the water, to the unknown. Realizing that things are not always in your control, you can do your best by focusing on those things that you do have control over, and be prepared, expecting there can be outcomes that will be different from any perfect plan.

Don't you think it makes sense to anchor to the unknown instead of anchoring to certainty?

I guess what you're saying is that when you're going to take action, or make a decision, the mindset should be one of knowing that not everything is in your control, you should not create false expectations which could set you up for disappointment. Plus, expecting deviations from your plan is more realistic and then you can be more prepared to shift or make changes.

Reflecting back on the clapper, what if each clack can be a reminder that life is uncertain? Each clack can be useful to greet that moment where the illusion of a straight line and perfection meet to remind us things can move in any direction.

—That's right. It's a choice.

You can either focus only on the outcome and make a decision based on whether it met your artificial illusion, or you can decide to maintain a mindset or a condition that keeps you aware that variation exists.

You're only human Robin, you can't control every outcome associated with your actions.

I agree. To your point, the adaptation you're talking about has to do with learning right? When something you plan for, or a decision you make doesn't come out as you "falsely" expected, when you have the flexible mindset you suggested, then you can choose to not freeze up, be defeated.

Use the outcome to check what did not go well and learn from that, for the next time.

—I agree, if people would only change their negative association of my name, and connect it with learning, then it would all be great. Less fear of trying things out and making decisions. They can move forward and not stay stuck.

That is great advice. We have the power to choose the relationship we want with you.

It's much better to choose not to have you as a foe, an enemy, and instead have you be a friend that is sharing valuable feedback with you so you can learn.

I'm thinking *you're* a *Friend* that gives *Feedback* for me to *Find* my way to success.

—Some very beautiful F words, I think. Robin.

"Success is not final, failure is not fatal: it is the courage to continue that counts."

Sir Winston Churchill

Interview:
Part 6

When we hear an F word it's typically associated with a bad thing. Including your name. The good thing is that it's not all F words.

So, I think I would make more emphasis on those that are associated with positive thoughts so we can use them to our benefit. Make them our friends, not our foes.

—I think you're on to something good Robin. Using words that are associated with good things to offset some of the negative misunderstandings of what I really am here to do for you.

Look, earlier in the interview we discussed that moving toward success requires a flexible mindset, and acknowledging that uncertainty is actually more practical, than certainty.

This is the basis for the attitude of the scientist who uses experiments as a way forward. The mere idea that you're running an experiment can give you the freedom to move forward.

It's all just trial and error for learning.

That's right. I've heard of so many scientists, and non-scientists that have found success through trying things out and adjusting the trials along the way. Some of them took many many trials, but in the end, they got something that was useful, to them and to others.

I'm thinking about how it took Edison as an inventor, 1,000 unsuccessful attempts at inventing the light bulb. Or the story of WD40 the spray lubricant. It took a team 40 attempts to get the WD water displacing formula worked out.

In both cases there was a lot of trial and error, many obstacles along the way, until they found success.

Success looks more like a curvy line.

—True. The important lesson in trial and error, is what to do with the errors along the way. Cause there will be many. What I have seen others do is to think of experiments as trials with the only expectation that there will be outcomes.

And that those outcomes are feedback that tells you whether you're on the right track, or not.

However, let me be clear, the feedback I'm talking about here is one coming directly out from your trials. Only actual observed results and outcomes can provide you true feedback.

Which means you have to take action.

Wanting, hopes, opinions or dreams without actually taking action will not provide you real outcomes that you can then compare against what you intended to achieve.

To me, real outcomes sounds so much like real friends. I just looked up a definition of a friend is : "a person one knows, likes or trusts." And another is "one who helps and supports."

I guess we can use these definitions to color the results we get from every trial. These are the true unbiased friends disguised as outcomes to provide you with candid feedback — not just friendly opinions.

For success to come about, you have to take action. And for the outcomes, you're not looking for "nice" or "polite" but instead an objective way to learn — you are running your trials to get to the next stage, closer and closer to your goal and you can only do this through the support of real, observed information created from the results of your trials.

Results are your true friends.

—Yes Robin, I think real, true Friendship will tell you things you may not like. Outcomes, as friends, can see past your shadow, and if you're truly open to see, listen and understand, you will continue with your experiment, always adjusting along the way based on the friendly feedback.

But I think there's one more F word worth talking about, and that is Faith.

Wow. That's a good one. I've never thought about Faith as part of this. Tell us more about how it can help?

—Consider that faith is not about religious beliefs. Instead think how faith has to do with curiosity and with

an openness to the mystery of unknown things to come. Realizing that things you don't necessarily already know, can in fact exist out there as new possibilities — that you may not be able to think about if you maintain a limited way of thinking.

This is the type of faith that provides you the power of resiliency: getting back on our feet when you fall. Faith in the knowing that after any outcome, you will have learned something that shows you the direction where to steer away from and where to move next.

Faith is an ingredient that when combined with friendship and feedback: creates a very powerful formula. One that can empower you to keep on trying, to continue to take action.

You cannot know for sure that things will turn out a certain way. But with faith, you know for sure that there will be an outcome and that from every outcome you will learn something.

Success exists through action and learning. It is however unpredictable and may come from many directions. You cannot know what will happen, but you can keep up the expectation that your action and its outcome will be helpful. Each step will show you which way not to take again, and help point you in the right direction.

Thank you for that! Just the thought that we are running an experiment is so helpful, but with the positive associations of friendship and faith, I think that really helps in removing the other F word, Fear, and the bad habit of postponing our actions. We can jump right, take action and move toward success.

—**Please let me share another story for your listeners Robin.**

A person is sitting on a fence.

They have one leg hanging to one side, the other leg to the other. They are observing both sides, thinking about what direction to take. Fence sitters often are great at calling out what they see as defects or problems, yet these are based on a limited perspective.

Or, perhaps, let's say it's an incomplete perspective.

Fence sitters tell them-selves a story about what's going on, on the left side of the fence and the right side of the fence. And because their world is clouded by right and left, their thoughts are influenced to think there is right and wrong, either or, all or nothing.

Left and right create thinking in polar opposites, ignoring a space that exists, the in-between of possibilities, the many shades of grey that exist between black and white.

The fence sitter is certainly influenced by the fence which seems to be splitting the world into two opposite sides. Yet the fence itself is neutral.

The interpretation of separate sides of an absolute

two-sided reality might also be influenced by their thoughts, and their thoughts are constructed by their words.

What is the fence sitter leaving out of the picture? What are they ignoring? What are they diminishing? What are they highlighting?

What words are keeping the fence sitter stuck, frozen and unable to move in either direction?

Perhaps it's words like *always* or *never* that help form the illusion of either or. But if you check in on how often things work in absolutes, you might realize that those words do not really represent reality.

I thought about something we can add to the fence.

It has a gate so the fence sitter can take responsibility and act as the gate keeper of what gets through and what doesn't. Meanings that are not useful can be kept out by thinking this way.

If we can control the gate this way, we can make it easy to take the first step which might not take me to my destination right away, but it sure can free me from where I'm stuck today, on the fence.

—Good!

Robin — Did you make breakfast or dinner yesterday? Did you drive yourself to work? Did you feed your pet? Were you successful in getting things done yesterday and earlier before we met?

Yes, I did all that. What is the question about?

—**What words were you using while doing those activities? Did the food come out perfect? Did you drive perfectly? Did you feed your pet perfectly? Perhaps you have a level of tolerance for smaller flubs and bloopers, but judge yourself on other things using other people's words?**

Do you mean it's hard to be a total complete failure when you notice that in between there are times when you get things done, and move on without ruminating about the meal, the drive or your pet?

—**Yes. Exactly.**

Let's check back in with the fence sitter, but this time let's widen the field of view on each side.

Like everything else in life, change is constant, so the fence is also on the move.

Looking to your left to the edge of as far as your eyes can see, toward the past, how far have you come? How many miles from the edge have you moved? How many meals and other successes have you achieved?

Notice how there are shades of grey in between the black and white thoughts. You've made some mistakes, but none have been fatal. You're still here. And along the

way you were unknowingly experimenting and gathered lessons and knowledge.

Reflect on the learning, it is yours to keep.

Now check the right side of the fence and look out to the edge of what your eyes can see, out into the future. You've come all this way, and now own all this knowledge and experience to support you on your next step.

What words have been keeping you from getting off the fence? If those words are not serving you, who is to say that you cannot create your own?

Creators create things that did not exists before. Once you label something in way that can serve you, it becomes alive and enters your thoughts.

You have brought something new into creation.

Anyone is able to label and create. Thank you.

This is a great first step to take and be a doer to move forward, not just judge from a fence and get passed by.

I think the listeners are getting a lot from your fence sitter story.

How much closer to white is the grey from where you're standing now?

How will you know you moved into the next space?

What will you notice is happening?

For my listeners: challenge yourself, accept you've never done this before, you're on your way, not there *yet*.

You're learning because you don't know this or that *yet*.

You're practicing and experimenting because you are not good at this or that *yet*.

"Perfect" closes the space and keep you frozen, on the fence, but, Yet — can help open up the space between black and white, right and wrong, either or, and all or nothing.

Buckle up! The best is Yet to come.

"Most people master the art of postponing the start."

Mokokoma Mokhonoana

Interview:
Part 7

I'm thinking we can move on to some ideas to continue creating a positive feeling around your name.

I think definitely the Friendship, Feedback and Faith trio are great ways to broaden our perspective. Do you have other ideas for our listeners?

—Yes, actually. I'll give you a few more. You may want to take notes.

In the past I've mentioned to people that in some other languages there are words that are my cousins, but they are less harsh, less fatalistic when dealing with something that doesn't come out right. For example, in Arabic, they use Fadeeja when a mistake is made but it has kind of a more human tone, sometimes even comical. And modern Hebrew also has a similar word it borrowed from Arabic: Fashla. When used it mostly implies *"to err is human"* which helps people not freeze up with fear, to move forward and take the first step.

After all, getting egg on your face is not fatal.

Fadeeja and Fashla. More F words? I think I'll start using those.

Flop and Flub are two more.

Would you recommend using antonyms or opposites to create positive associations about you?

—Well, it depends. First, I think we should clarify how to deal with how some folks see as opposites. I mentioned earlier how black and white are not necessarily opposites, but people often refer to these two distinct and unique colors as if they were contraries. Think about it, black is black and white is white, each is a specific hue that vibrates at a unique frequency. Humans have made these opposites, but they are independently unique. The point is that the use of black and white as opposites is a lazy comparison to refer to what is absolute, as in right and wrong, implying that there are only two possible options. That is kind of rigid don't you think?

I see your point. I guess thinking that way we limit to an *all or nothing* way of thinking. Thinking we have only two options can create lots of fear and anxiety to move forward. We might be closing a lot of doors when we do that, when what we really want is to open as many doors as possible, but without fear.

I noted here your point about "lazy comparison". Are you saying that in the way we choose to speak we are lazy?

—Not in a negative sense. Lazy is a normal human condition Robin, intended to help save energy. Remember that you have an ancient brain that is still catching up from the time that it wasn't so easy to ensure food for the day, or that you would not be eaten by a wild animal. But that is a conversation for another time.

Here's another way of putting it. Think about a centipede. What comes to mind?

A caterpillar with 100 feet?

—Yes, that is the idea. But I am quite sure that not every centipede has exactly 100 feet. I also don't think that whoever inserted the centipede word in a dictionary counted feet. I think it's a convenient, lazy way to give a name to something. Here's the thing, the word centi means 100, which is an absolute number. But a centipede is not an absolute entity, each one may have more or less feet.

The point is words don't necessarily match reality. They are not absolute truths.

Perhaps using the idea of 100 was a shortcut, to generalize a species and not have to worry about each specific caterpillar to have to name it differently.

This lazy way to name things could also become a problem when a word is being spoken by the voice in your head that implies an absolute, right and wrong, one and only truth.

What incredible examples. Thank you.

Sorry, I was thinking about millipedes, where milli is 1,000 and who would have sat down to count if they each have 1,000 feet ha ha. An even bigger absolute number that doesn't match the actual real caterpillar.

But seriously, with your way of opening the idea to challenge the meaning we thought was absolute, I'm thinking it's also about our lazy convenient way to think of opposites of words.

For example, night and day are really not opposites if you consider each is a unique domain, with independent characteristics. Humans decided to label night when the sun sets, and day when it rises.

But what about dusk and dawn? When exactly does dusk end for night to begin? When does dawn begin and when does it end to let the day begin?

So again, no absolute. Just a convenient way to refer to each, and use them as opposites.

—There you go Robin. And there is an even bigger issue from your example of night and day.

Remember, the sun does not rise, and it doesn't set. It's the earth, with humans on it that moves around the sun.

The rising and setting is an illusion that you have chosen to latch on to and believe to be true, maybe you labeled it so for convenience. Like many other things that you choose to believe to be true that hold you back and limit your experience.

Look, another example of that is the meme going around about an optimist labeled as one who sees a glass

half full, and a pessimist as someone who see the glass half empty. The same problem is present here with that way of limited thinking because it implies absolutes.

What I mean is that unless someone is measuring the exact halfway mark on the glass, based on the actual volume of the glass, then the half empty or half full are abstract concepts, not real.

Good point, and funny too because wouldn't that mean if the glass is less than half full, it would define a partial pessimist, and a half empty glass a partial optimist? Or even better mean that an optimist is not always an optimist and a pessimist is not always a pessimist.

And by the way, is it correct to even label the empty half, empty?

I seem to recall from my science class that air is present on top of the liquid in the glass, we don't see it but it's there. And thankfully so, because we need air to breath.

So, the word empty is also not an adequate label in that description.

—Brilliant. I'm quite optimistic by now that your listeners will want to choose a word that can be useful to them, and replace mine.

"Emptiness is the absence of some things, not the absence of everything."

Mokokoma Mokhonoana

Interview:
Part 8

Do you suggest a certain way or process for someone to choose a better meaning of your name? what are the steps?

—Robin, I think before that it will be important for your listeners to get a grasp on the way words actually work. Remember, you don't just want to choose a random word, or random sound that doesn't sound like something useful or beneficial. Look, there are many other words written down beside mine on so many pages in the dictionary that share a problem. The problem is that the definitions of some words are written by people, humans, based on descriptions they may hold of their own or even general feelings that others have shared. But that doesn't mean their definitions are the only definitions. If I talk to you about love for example, the dictionary will have a definition, but love for you can mean something different than the description.

Here is another way to think about this.

Imagine you're up and about at the end of the day, when the glow of the sun has not gotten away even for a moment.

Then, inevitably, darkness stumbles in as it has always done, slowly creeping and taking over what was left of a well-lit sky.

In this changing of the guard, a star is now visible.

Then another and another, flickering away independently, each at their whim and pace.

And all the while, the flickering persists with the intention of attracting and being noticed.

Each star is incessantly competing for your attention.

In this magical light show, can you see how others before you, a long time ago, felt invited to play with the dots and connected them, to form shapes of animals, objects and even deities to work up stories to tell others.

They gave birth to imaginary constellations and made-up stories with random connections.

Andromeda, Aries and Cassiopeia, in a play with Aquarius, Musca and Orion. Made-up, fantasy connections suddenly formed stories and those stories told often, formed beliefs.

What do you think Robin?

I always thought the idea of constellations was kind of silly because stars are not on a 2-dimensional plane. When we look at the sky, we think we are seeing a flat screen but it's more like 3D, there is depth between the stars. So straight lines were just imaginary, you could draw an image of a constellation on a piece of paper, but it really did not reflect reality. Sorry for you Orion, you're just an illusion too.

In any case, I guess before television and social media, such made-up stories and constellations of flickering objects inspired great nighttime entertainment. It can be just for fun.

So, I guess we can still decide on our own new constellations by connecting our own dots. Hey, with so many possible combinations of stars, there's probably an infinite number of constellations that can be brought to existence.

—Yes, Robin exactly. Naming something brings it into awareness, it gives it life.

Going back to the sunrise and sunset you brought up earlier. Have you ever been in a situation, on a mountain or at the ocean, where the sun was setting, and in the moment, you had a feeling of awe, beauty, amazement?

Yes, sure. It makes me feel warm, a meaning for life.

It's like, wow, unreal.

—Well, that very moment, with yourself, is an ineffable moment, an emotional moment, it's abstract and difficult to name with just one word, right?

That is right.

—I like your comment of "unreal".

Because while reality is happening out there, in nature, inside your head at that moment you have no words that would help place that moment on a map of reality. The feeling is inexpressible. It's beyond words.

But then, you meet up with your friends or family, and

you want to share the experience of that moment, and your head then turns on the button that searches for a word that can help you convey to others what you felt.

So, you're talking again about words as tools? Tools for humans to share and communicate with others. I guess what you're implying is that some things cannot be named, or labeled in a way they would make sense to everyone the same way?

—Right, think of how you were feeling the sunset moment compared to how you were thinking when you tried to express your unspeakable experience to others. In my world, us words, we come to life when you're trying to move from an abstract concept, a feeling, to something concrete and that's when we come to your rescue.

Thinking is done using words. Thought is structured by the words you choose, and these words are living somewhere in your memory. You stored them there at a particular moment, under particular circumstances that presented themselves in your life. That's also why you can refer to what you're doing as a re-presentation of your feeling of the sunset.

Presenting to others using words from the past.

OK, I think I get it. The words we choose preexist somewhere in the past. They don't necessarily express every new moment we experience. There will be differences, yet we are somehow limited because not everything can be described accurately, precisely.

I can see how this relates to my question about choosing a word that is useful to replace your name. Because based on their own circumstances when they acquired and saved the word into their memory, the word will have a unique meaning, that does not match yours?

—Yes, that is partially what I'm trying to build up to so your listeners can get a good idea about what is needed. In my case for example, even though there are written definitions of my name, I'm more inclined to think that my name is really a platitude. I get used so often, I don't really harness interest because it may be used as a profound idea, but it really has no depth. It cannot have depth because it is subjective, where different people have different meanings about me. A platitude like love, or success cannot be measured the same way by you and each and every one of your listeners.

You're saying that we should come up with a meaning that can be measurable or concrete. A meaning that can be understood the same way by others because there is an objective way to quantify what it means. Like when we can take a measuring tape that shows inches or centimeters, and two or more people can agree on what 36 inches looks like. You can re-present the 36 inches by making a reference to the tape measure. But there is no tape measure to measure your name, or success for that matter?

—Yes, in the case of that old aunt declaring to your dad that he was a total failure. How was your aunt measuring failure? Based on what reference point, what tape measure? She and your dad could've opened a discussion to establish specifically how she came to her conclusion and that could've been quite interesting, had they been able to reach an agreement about the meaning of my name in a particular situation.

Wait, I thought you were saying the word should be unique and useful to each individual. I'm a bit confused why define a measurable way as if two people need to agree on the meaning?

—Good question Robin. It would be great if others share the same meaning, but this may not be as easy.

However, for your listeners, the definition they should be thinking of is a personal one. How they choose to define and measure the meaning of my name so they can hold themselves accountable. Without a defined measure, trial and error might take place in a random, unstructured way.

That personal agreement is what will make it solid and concrete for them and then it would truly become useful.

This is really, really good. A personal agreement on the unique new meaning of your name. Each person chooses for themselves, but also agrees on how to measure. The new word or a new meaning can then become the guiding principle to help move forward. And there's no need to share it with anyone or make it public. It's there to support you, to be useful, that serves you when you need it.

It sounds like it's about making a silent accord.

"An expert is a person who has made all the mistakes that can be made in a very narrow field."

Niels Bohr

Interview:
Part 9

What can you suggest to our listeners that want to make a great silent accord?

—**Well, perhaps we go back to the part where we were talking about perfection, where we said it doesn't exist. Since you brought up the "silent accord" idea Robin, why not start out by strengthening the fact that perfection is a self-imposed, a self-created standard and it's imposed by something inside of you.**

When people talk about an inner critic, it's usually very focused on the negative. That "critic" calls you out about how you "should have" done something, or what you did not do right. That critic is acting as an obstacle blocking you from seeing what you were meant to learn from your actions.

Can you see how this applies to someone's silent accord?

I think it can be used in a couple of ways.

One is to make a silent accord accepting that since perfection is an illusion, whatever we achieve will not measure based on an imaginary standard. We can instead define our own standard; one that keeps us going, seeking the next step and then the next.

It's like not letting a word limit how we see things as either or.

The other is a result of completely rejecting the existence

of perfection, which opens one up to a sense of extreme curiosity and adventure. It can give you the power of resiliency and the energy to continue onward.

Then we get to have more choices.

—Those are good, really good. If I can add some more to yours, so the listeners can have more ideas, while you were talking I had the sense about the energy of resiliency and curiosity to move forward continuously, like water flowing downstream no matter what gets in the way.

Water will go through and around obstacles with a natural flexibility. Remember, the term "the situation is very fluid" means it's always subject to change in an unpredictable way, but always moving. I'd say this term is so close to reality, folks should use it more often.

There it is then folks, three ideas that can help guide your silent accord:

1. Perfection is an illusion, define a realistic standard to measure your actions.

2. Adopt an attitude of extreme curiosity, and

3. Think and act like water: reality is always fluid.

Come to think of it, there may be some other things we can add to the attitude part because folks are realizing that attitude has a lot to do with how we feel and how we react.

For example, considering perfection is an illusion, we can make the choice of how we react to something when it does not go the way we wanted it to. It really didn't have to go our way in the first place.

It was simply wanting, and wanting doesn't guarantee anything.

Or also by thinking it would have been better if it had resulted like this or that, but realizing the outcome is inconvenient, but not awful, or fatal.

Sometimes when I'm disappointed with a result, I've replaced the words *terrible* and *unbearable* with *inconvenient* and *uncomfortable*, or *unfortunate* and *unpleasant* — which are probably closer to reality, since the situation was not life-threatening or terminal.

When I do that, it helps me refocus to keep on moving, as you suggest- staying fluid. I guess thinking this way opens a space, where perfection cannot exist. The words sound a bit less end-of-the-world-there's-nothing-I-can-do which help me realize in the moment I can just do my very best, but not the impossible.

Choosing such alternate words has helped me realize that my desires are random, just self-invented, so if I demand that things go my way it's kind of silly. What do you think about these ideas?

—They can be very helpful and very powerful. Notice again how words drive thinking? Attitude shifts from end-of-the-world thinking to bearable enough, allowing one to move forward.

Remove power from the words that close your space.

Give power to the words that open your space.

What I think makes good sense is for people to hit the pause button and reflect a bit instead of running like crazy. You can actually pause the "it is so", or "has to be like that", which will open a space for other ideas and for learning.

And one more thing, once the attitude changes to learning, then your comment about curiosity is very important Robin, because the openness to *anything — is — possible* helps fuel the cycle of learning which is ultimately a key ingredient for success.

Very good advice indeed. Seems like we are covering a lot of ideas for our listeners to build their own, silent accord that can help propel them forward. A couple of things that resonated with me is that the fluidity you mentioned resembles a process, one that never stops and is continual, fueled by the attitude of learning and curiosity. So, it's not a static one-time issue. It's all very dynamic.

And also, the *anything — is — possible* attitude helped me visualize a different picture of how success can be reimagined.

Often, we see success as stairs or a ladder moving in a

straight line from the bottom to the top, where the top is success. But I think your idea is more about moving one step ahead, experimenting and allowing each step to go in any direction and then learn about the outcome, and why it ended up in that direction. Then, we can use what was learned to go to the next step and so on.

The direction can be zig zag, diagonal, or squiggly.

Straight up sounds a lot like an ill-formed expectation, and we already talked about that.

—Let's say Robin that instead of just a process and a goal, the silent accord might be about sustaining a condition, a way of thinking or mindset from where the journey to success flows without end. That state of mind or condition is what can help connect the dots. It considers that change is constant, things are continuously being created and recreated, therefore experimentation is the way to move forward by learning with each trial.

"The road to success is always under construction."

Chinese Proverb

Interview:
Part 10

Brilliant, we have to drink water every day. That should help remind us of the fluid state of mind. Achieving that state in itself can be a great measure of success. Thank you for that.

What would you say to our listeners about success? What ideas can you share that can help them add to their silent accord?

—Well it's good that you mentioned earlier that success is not the opposite of my name, mainly because it's not really helpful to think in opposites because they reduce the choices you have. People think if A is happening the B can't possibly exist, or if A wins then B must lose. Even though you have made these artificial divisions of A and B in your mind, those imaginary thoughts then create the lens by which you see and judge things.

So, it's important to open the space up to multiple ways things can result that you can identify and call success.

I guess what you're saying is that success can have many faces? And we should then move past any preconceived notions limited by either or, and instead choose a definition that leaves the door open to a range of possibilities. I'm thinking that unfortunately in the social media today there is an extreme bias toward success equaling having a lot of money, but I also see where people talk about other priorities like health, family, friends and community. How do you see that?

—Sure, Robin, and each person will have to decide what is important to them, what they really value and build their own priority list to define what to include in their unique silent accord. For example, someone can put health over money, because without health it can be tough to have the energy to do what it takes to earn more money, or run a business.

By the way, over time your list of values can change, just like everything else is in constant change. So, today you might write family at the top of your priority list, and later that can change to health or community. What is important is that you choose the list and use it as your guiding principle that you choose to make your foundation. That's what will keep you moving forward.

I just googled a couple of definitions of success, and am thinking those were also written by a bunch of grumpy old men and we can change the meaning to what is useful for each of us. For example, one online definition is *"the fact of getting or achieving wealth, respect, or fame"*. But now after your comments, I think I would want to think this one through. These sound like there is a preestablished measure of what is being valued by others, but not be valued by you.

The other problem is that it is limited to getting and achieving wealth, or respect or fame, but these are I think very subjective. Is fame about being recognized when you're walking the street? How would you measure respect? Someone kissing your ring? Or how much money do you have to have to consider you achieved wealth. I've had millionaires on my show who've admitted they are not there yet, and are still looking for success.

—That's right Robin, and I can't tell you how many seemingly wealthy people are so afraid of my name. Some of them fear losing it all, some of them fear having criminals look for opportunities to rob them, or the government coming after them. They also associate my name with fear of losing some of their huge wealth. Others might see them as successful, but under certain circumstances, they might not be? If they are stressed out and not healthy and have to be under a doctor's constant supervision, or if they have family feuds about money. Or when love in their lives is only about their bank account? I think instead it's about a process, an individual mindset and set of values and principles that can help support a definition of success to help define their own personal and unique silent accord.

Ok this is great. If it's a mindset, and the focus is not on a specific predefined outcome, then I'm thinking that what has been helpful for me are a few things that keep me moving forward, and that I can relate to as my personal way of seeing success. For example: I think I'm an optimist when I set myself to think that learning is one of the most important things for me. Then, no matter the outcome, I know I will learn something from it that will lead me into the next step.

So, in a sense, I'm thinking step by step, but also reaching milestones that I can use to find out what to not continue doing and think of alternatives of where to next. That is one way I think to help define success as a process that creates the opportunity to learn and improve at each milestone.

—Yes, that is a good one. I think your optimism also helps solidify the idea of harnessing faith that things will resolve themselves, that obstacles and challenges are there not to be bad-asses, instead think how they are there to create the opportunity to learn. When you don't see obstacles as threats, the mindset will keep you curious, thirsty to continue learning. And then, the more you learn and realize the importance of learning, will give you even more confidence to continue to the next milestone.

I know that I sound like a broken record, but it's better to define success as a target condition or mindset, a way of thinking, not a specific goal or final outcome.

I agree, that is a better way. I guess it also implies that obstacles that appear along the way, the same ones that cause straight lines to go squiggly can also be bringing with them some gifts.

Opportunities can come from any direction, we just have to have the mindset to be aware so we can see them.

I mean, what if what you're trying to avoid might actually bring you success?

But I think it also helps silence that inner critic, the voice in your head that attacks you when something comes out seemingly wrong. It's only judging you against a static one-time target, but not a moving process that is deliberately designed to make you succeed. It's that self-talk, that we should get rid of once and for all.

—Well not so fast. That self-talk is there for a reason Robin, to somehow protect you from hurting yourself. It's just that the voice might have been trained for either or situations, A or B, right or wrong. Perhaps you can one day retrain that parrot. But, getting rid of it is not a good idea. It might transform into a shadow which you won't see but can still influence you.

Here is a different way you may consider. Let the inner critic challenge the outcomes of your experiments. In other words, it's judging the outcome and not you. Then the conversation is no longer a personal one.

Why not just call it shelf talk? Put it on a shelf, it will be there when you're ready to explore the way forward.

Shelf talk, that's funny. I'll do it.

"We shape our buildings and afterwards our buildings shape us."

Sir Winston Churchill

Interview: *Part 11*

We're coming up to the time slotted for our interview. I think the listeners have gained some great insight about you, hopefully a different perspective that can help them move on, be less afraid, let go and move forward. I'm sensing you have more to give us? Before we go, do you have some additional tips and ideas you'd like to share?

—Sure, I have some more, but I think for your listeners it would be worthwhile to share a word that I think could help them a lot. Also because it has been used in theater and movies and many people have heard it but may not know how it can help remove fear.

That word is Oz, like from the Wizard of Oz. Have you watched the movie or the play?

Yes, actually it is a favorite of mine. But I've not looked into the Oz word. What is it?

—In ancient biblical Hebrew, the word Oz is associated with courage and also the strength to dare do something you haven't done before. This two-letter word can have enormous power to help people lose or reduce their fear of my name. Such power could for example give people the courage to move ahead and define their own version of success, which would shift their mindset to one that allows them to learn and grow. By channeling oz, people can also

feel at ease to return any borrowed words that don't serve them well to whomever they got them from.

Does this make sense Robin?

Oh yes, absolutely. In a sense, Oz is empowering people to make choices about words that serve them and by solidifying their individuality, by blocking external negative influences that fuel their beliefs about success.

—And also, it can help people avoid remorse or perhaps guilt about choices they made in the past. Oz can help them understand that choices you made in the past were made from a different mindset and under a different set of circumstances. Circumstances change all the time, nothing remains static, and no one has to carry guilt and then associate it with my name.

But I think this is where Oz works best: by taking action and trying new things and learning from those unexpected outcomes you're moving past what you thought were obstacles. Then, once you're on the other side of that obstacle, looking back, you suddenly realize that the obstacle looked tougher at the time, than it really was.

You took that step, you earned more Oz. Then you move one step forward, again.

Thank you, that is really helpful you know, I myself tend to carry my past with me and it sometimes drags me down. I'll take your tip and start using Oz a lot more. Since you brought up the tale of the Wizard of Oz, I was thinking we can also adapt your idea of courage and daring to help us find out why the obstacle seems a lot bigger than it really is?

I feel sometimes like someone has cast a spell on me that prevents me from taking a leap I know would allow me to learn and grow.

Like trying to see who the wizard behind the curtain is that is casting the spell?

—Certainly. That is a worthwhile idea. Why don't we go ahead and do that right now?

Close your eyes Robin.

Pretend there is a curtain in front of you, right there where you are.

Go ahead and remember the things we've been discussing about words, how their meaning sits in your head and not in the word, how dictionary meanings can be random or arbitrary and how different people can carry different meanings of the same word, how perfection is an illusion.

Now, knowing all this, go ahead Robin and imagine you're pulling back the curtain. What do you see?

[PAUSE.]

OMG. I pulled back the curtain there's nothing there. Whatever it is, it's totally invisible. Does that mean? Wait.

The spell is gone.

Failure is not what it used to be.

[SILENCE.]

There you have it folks. I hope today's podcast was valuable today, I sure learned a few things and will go back through my notes to make sure I integrate these ideas into my journey.

As always, you can download the transcript from my website.

I look forward to your comments and feedback which I will definitely use as input for a future episode, and they will also be up on the website blog in case you want to check them out.

Thank you for joining today and hope to see you on my next episode.

Hey, guess what, I'm going to try to get Perfection on one of my shows.

In the meantime,

Stay tuned.

The video call ended abruptly. Robin could not reconnect to thank Failure for being available for the interview.

He turned off his laptop and walked over to his bookshelf to find his old college English language dictionary, scrolled and opened page 178, where he found a word he no longer had use for, and ripped the page out.

"When I was a little kid, I was really scared of the dark. But then I came to understand, dark just means the absence of photons in the visible wavelength — 400 to 700 nanometers. Then I thought, well, it's really silly to be afraid of a lack of photons. Then I wasn't afraid of the dark anymore after that."

Elon Musk

The single biggest problem with
Failure, is the illusion that it exists.*

*Yes, the original quote attributed to George Bernard Shaw
is about communication. I just adapted it slightly.

Afterword:
a brief explanation from the author

The story, so far — but don't take my word for it.

When I was a kid, my father used to tease me and scare the living daylights out of me by chanting repeatedly: "El palo, las escoba y la bruja ..." (the stick, the broom and the witch), which would petrify me until I cried. I don't remember much else from those days, but I can still hear the sound of those words reverberating in my head, as my dad chased me around the house.

I had managed to create my very own horror images from someone else's words. Even though there was no real evidence of a broomstick and no witch anywhere near, I believed my own terrifying imagination.

My dad's words had secretly seeped below the surface, covertly shading the way I saw the world.

A shadow had been created, lurking, until the right moment to show up disguised as a voice. When I hoped for an inner mentor to come to the rescue, a tormentor showed up instead, loudly uttering through a mega horn.

I was all ears to that voice that highjacked my thoughts.

Like in my case, parents and other people we trusted in our childhood may have used words in ways they interpreted as useful, with positive intention. You trusted so much, you did not challenge.

I imagine in their experience and upbringing, they inherited meanings that were at the time socially and culturally accepted which formed their unique model of the world, and their story.

In the end, it was their story, not mine.

Luckily, my professional training in continuous improvement and quality, allowed me to create a different meaning of the F word, based partially on my experience, mostly about experiments.

I start with a theory, plan an experiment to prove it out objectively, take the step to try it, pause to reflect and learn what worked and what didn't according to the theory, use the new knowledge to make more experiments.

Besides, as a multilingual nerd, I love to look up words and their origins. When I realized the F word came from the 12th century, I figured it's time to check in how things looked back then and if they still relate to any of our 21st century reality.

Over 800 years later, the internet, globalization, and great migrations have brought radical and fundamental changes to our cultures and mindsets.

We update our mobile phones, operating systems and security software.

Is it time for the next update of the F word?

Remember also that a word cannot define you. Your story and your identity are not made up by one single factor. You are much more complex than that and made up of numerous different features.

Shadows tend to dissipate when we cast light on them.

I believe that a useful, well thought out meaning can be that light.

In the book, I tried to share a few ideas for you to use to find that light and edit your story. But I do not prescribe or dictate what you should or shouldn't do, the ideas are really about adding choices to your life.

Some of us are unsuspecting contributors when we decide to accept someone's gift even when it doesn't benefit us, yet still chose to keep it and make it ours.

What if you realized you can be the custodian of your thoughts, by deliberately defining the meanings that color the words that you know are kicking your butt?

It would be like turning the tables: you hijacking your inner critic's voice when you need to.

Language is a human invention meant to help people interact and commune with others. What we often ignore is a side effect of language, when some words used to communicate with others have a different impact when we communicate with our selves.

In his book *Rich Dad, Poor Dad* Robert T. Kiyosaki wrote:

"It's not what you say out of your mouth that determines your life, it's what you whisper to yourself that has the most power!"

I bet we spend way more time "whispering" to ourselves with other people's words — than the time we spend talking to others. That quote reminded me to be aware of the words in my whispers because those have the most power. Remember, words become the lenses through which you observe reality, but they are not reality.

Words seed your thoughts. Thoughts generate your beliefs. Beliefs drive your actions.

Thus, communication pre-seeds your actions.

In many cases, there's no need to look any further, especially to just take the first step: words are tools you carry with you all the time.

You don't have to be a rapper. Anyone can invent a word or change a meaning, or choose which words they'd like to retire. But be sure to take responsibility and choose meanings that in your self-talk will help steer you in the right direction.

Check in on the meanings of the words you use today and invent new ones along the way to keep you moving forward to success.

Curious about new and retired words? Google: "new English words added to dictionary" or "words deleted from the dictionary."

On a personal note, another F word is Feeding. I've been so strict with what I feed myself because of my food sensitivities: lactose and gluten intolerances, I strive to be intolerant, by choice, to words that don't suit me. After all they say, you are what you eat.

* * *

Now, back to when I was a kid.

I can't possibly remember exactly, but I suspect that after crawling for a while, I started to try to walk. I stumbled, fell and tried to get up. Then I did that again until finally I took my first step.

By then, the F word had been coined by grumpy old men yet sat tucked away in the middle of a page in a dictionary on a bookshelf. It had no effect on my motivation to learn how to walk.

I quickly learned about gravity, without knowing it by name. I now think it was there to provide feedback, as a friend, and gave me the faith to be curious and take the first step. Then the next, and the next after that, until I was upright waddling around. Dr. Martin Luther King once said: "Faith is taking the first step, even if you don't see the whole staircase."

You too can discreate the meaning you unknowingly accepted, if you remember the learning-to-walk mindset, take the first step, and change your story.

Thank you for reading my 25th draft. It's not perfect.

I started writing this book as a novel several years ago, but it wasn't ready yet, so I set it aside always wanting to get back to finish what I started.

Recently, after the COVID-19 pandemic, I found the discipline to resume writing, in a voice that I was able to now. (Until I learn to write novels.)

Writing is an incredible exercise that connects ideas and thoughts in your brain and brings them to life when they get put into words on paper or your favorite electronic document.

Considering the F theme and the main character, I've strived to provide you, the reader, with ideas and analogies that can help you in your journey and motivate you to take your first step.

The ideas are interpretations from my experiences in life and work, reading, reflecting, and teaching.

There is an abundance of literature, videos and podcasts that will help you complement these ideas. Gaining more intellectual knowledge is important but, in my opinion, is not enough to move you forward.

Plan, try, err, learn, reflect, learn some more and try again. Revisit your plan and try again.

Doing and feeling is what will leave the mark of transformation toward growth and success.

Since I think success has no deadline, I'm publishing the manuscript as is. I'll try, err, reflect and learn some more. Then, I'll probably edit this latest draft and publish Take 26, learn from your feedback and publish again.

In the meantime, if this version has helped you, or perhaps someone you know to take one step forward, my mission is accomplished.

What's my silent accord? I'm too old to grow up, too young to stop learning, delighted to share and give back.

* * *

Remember what the great Napoleon Hill said : "*Do not wait; the time will never be 'just right'. Start where you stand, and work with whatever tools you may have at your command, and better tools will be found as you go along.*"

Cheers and CLACK away y'all!
Thank you!
Sam.

Inspired and written while in:
Greenville, SC — USA
Eastbourne, England
San Diego, CA — USA

"The happiness of your life depends on the quality of your thoughts; therefore, guard accordingly."

Marcus Aurelius

Appendix 1:
a brief etymology and origins of the word

First Known Use of failure

https://www.merriam-webster.com/dictionary/failure#h1

1643, in the meaning defined at sense 1a:

Definition of failure

1a: omission of occurrence or performance *specifically* **:** a failing to perform a duty or expected action *failure* to pay the rent on time

First Known Use of fail

https://www.merriam-webster.com/dictionary/fail#h1

Verb

13th century, in the meaning defined at intransitive sense 1a

Definition of *fail* (Entry 1 of 2)

intransitive verb

1a: to lose strength **:** WEAKEN her health was *failing*

Noun

13th century, in the meaning defined at sense 1

Definition of *fail* (Entry 2 of 2)

1: FAILURE — usually used in the phrase *without fail* Every day, without *fail*, he has toast and coffee for breakfast.

Etymology:

https://www.etymonline.com/word/failure

failure (n.)

1640s, failer, "a failing, deficiency," also "act of failing," from Anglo-French failer, Old French falir "be lacking; not succeed" (see fail (v.)). The verb in Anglo-French used as a noun; ending altered 17c. in English to conform with words in -ure. Meaning "thing or person considered as a failure" is from 1837.

Entries linking to failure

fail (v.)

c. 1200, "be unsuccessful in accomplishing a purpose;" also "cease to exist or to function, come to an end;" early 13c. as "fail in expectation or performance," from Old French falir "be lacking, miss, not succeed; run out, come to an end; err, make a mistake; be dying; let down, disappoint" (11c., Modern French faillir), from Vulgar Latin *fallire, from Latin fallere "to trip, cause to fall;" figuratively "to deceive, trick, dupe, cheat, elude; fail, be lacking or defective." De Vaan traces this to a PIE root meaning "to stumble" (source also of Sanskrit skhalate "to stumble, fail;" Middle Persian škarwidan "to stumble, stagger;" Greek sphallein "to bring or throw down," sphallomai "to fall;" Armenian sxalem "to stumble, fail"). If so, the Latin sense is a metaphorical shift from "stumble" to "deceive." Related: Failed; failing.

Replaced Old English abreoðan. From c. 1200 as "be unsuccessful in accomplishing a purpose;" also "cease to exist or to function, come to an end;" early 13c. as "fail in expectation or performance."

From mid-13c. of food, goods, etc., "to run short in supply, be used up;" from c. 1300 of crops, seeds, land. From c. 1300 of strength, spirits, courage, etc., "suffer loss of vigor; grow feeble;" from mid-14c. of persons. From late 14c. of material objects, "break down, go to pieces."

-ure
suffix forming abstract nouns of action, from Old French -ure, from Latin -ura, an ending of fem. nouns denoting employment or result.

fail (n.)
late 13c., "failure, deficiency" (as in without fail), from Old French faile "deficiency," from falir (see fail (v.)). The Anglo-French form of the verb, failer, also came to be used as a noun, hence failure.

Appendix 2

Since a main theme of this book is *choice*, I tried the best possible to not imply everyone should do this or that. I felt the conversation should leave an opening for anyone to make their own choice whether to retire the word Failure, make up a new word or just associate a different meaning to it. I mentioned Friendship and Feedback which have been quite powerful for me.

In any case, here's a short list (thanks to Nancy Gooch) of other F words that anyone can use to either replace the word or associate it with a different meaning.

Friends	Freedom	Fluid
Flexibility	Faith	Flop
Feedback	Fall	Fuel
Freeze	Fatal	Foundation
Fear	First Step	Find
Forward	Flub	

Have fun connecting these words on a sheet of paper and making combinations, like: Fuelearn, FriendFall, Faithlearn, Flearn, Learnstep, Learnfriend — And of course, they don't have to be F words.

Scribble some of your words and combinations here:

131

Appendix 3

This is what I found when I looked up the origins of the word in French Faillir and listed several below. I also added the link in case another nerd like me wants to check it out.

https://artflsrv03.uchicago.edu/philologic4/publicdicos
/query?report=bibliography&head=faillir
His memory failed him.

This horse is beginning to fail in the legs.
I will go there without fail.
Failing and not going straight.
Failing to speak.
Failing to follow a pattern.
As in: To be mistaken, to misunderstand something.
To fail in promise.
Fail to rescue something or someone.
Failed to arrive on time.
We fail and make a mistake,
You failed: you must not have heard us correctly.
They failed to kill him.
He failed to become a senator.
She failed to hurt me.
The misfortune that failed to
This event failed to delay our departure.
Money fails us by the way
The most learned are liable to fail.

This Architect, this Painter, this Sculptor, have failed in the
  proportions.
It is a human thing to fail.
This author has failed in many places.
This author failed to see so many other choices.
I can fail, I am human.
Who cannot fail?

Appendix 4:
my experiment with real writing

When you get to the edge of the ocean, you might notice it's not blue.

Perhaps some is. Not all of it. Not always.

Not the image you've been carrying in your mind about the ocean.

You pause and witness, it's not just one color, there are many colors. Some out towards the deep, while others floating in closer to the shore.

And even more colors are mixing with each wave, as it forms, as it crests, and just as it crashes and splashes on the rocks and sand.

Brown, green, grey, bone with of sparks of silver white.

Reflections from the sky above blending and fusing with the elements below.

Like the artist thins out and blends paints, if you really pay attention, you'll notice other colors stirred by the mysterious energy source of tides that blends the hues, tones and tints.

An eternal, never ending dance of a universe of colors being created, from one moment to the next.

Dark hues, reflective silvers, greens, and shiny whites, playing in harmony with every other color.

It is indeed a color-full ocean.

That brief spark of fleeting blue is there to remind us that blue is not alone.

There's more than one story.

That blue is not the only, single truth. That other truths exist.

An infinite number of truths, swimming together, in harmony with each other.

Observe the waves, the tides, the water temperature, always in motion that never a pauses fueling continuous action that never stops.

Transforming and changing, constantly, continually, and persistently.

Old colors, becoming new colors, new waves replace recent waves.

You're witnessing endless experiments.

Experimentation never stops.

Stopping is not an option.

But pausing to reflect, is part of the creation process.

To create is to Think.... Experiment.... Reflect.... Assimilate.... Integrate.... Act.... Think again....

Thinking AND acting is creation.

Thoughts, like waves colliding with the status quo to trans-form old into new.

With boundless curiosity, the ocean tests the salt, water, temperature, currents, sun, moon, blending, fish, corals, invisible creatures and humans, infinite participants with infinite possibilities.

As the waterman pours the salt, above the clouds the beings control the rain, the weight of the sky moves the air and awakens the horizon to shake the waters into waves. Then the ocean reaches its deserved saltiness, the sun warms and the moon cools.

From every experiment, there's always a result — with a gift: learning something new, creating to continuously improve is the action.

Learning with each take.

The experiment always works: This is not the way, so try a different way.

Suddenly, a sun flare cracks the sky, and the tremors from the thunder of a thousand seagulls shake an angel off the clouds.

The angel plunges into the water, the Tsunami splashes the earth and clears the deck.

Clack! it's time to start over. The slate is clean.

What will your next step be?

Yes, the world needs you.

If not now when?

If not you, then who?

About the Author

Sam Yankelevitch is a former global operations executive, turned author, consultant, and international speaker. Based on his work with teams across the globe, he has developed ways for people to improve communication to succeed in the increasing complexity of the 21st century.

After having successfully written four non-fiction books, Sam decided it was time to share valuable insights about learning from trial and error which he gained through his professional and personal life experiences. *An Interview with Failure* is his first fiction book.

He is also a Linkedin Learning instructor, with several courses developed for project managers, supply chain professionals and operations personnel to improve human interactions needed to get the job done.

Sam insists he is too old to grow up, too young to stop learning and is delighted to give back and share.

Join Sam on Linkedin to start a conversation.
LinkedIn.com/in/samyankelevitch

Find Sam on his webiste:
SamYankelevitch.com

Other books by Sam Yankelevitch

Walking the Invisible Gemba

Lean Potion #9- Communication: The Next Lean Frontier

*Lean Communication: Applications for
Continuous Process Improvement*

*Global Lean: Seeing the New Waste Rooted in Communication,
Distance and Culture*